Dear Parent:
Your child's love of reading starts here!

Every child learns to read in a different way and at his or her own speed. Some go back and forth between reading levels and read favorite books again and again. Others read through each level in order. You can help your young reader improve and become more confident by encouraging his or her own interests and abilities. From books your child reads with you to the first books he or she reads alone, there are I Can Read Books for every stage of reading:

SHARED READING
Basic language, word repetition, and whimsical illustrations, ideal for sharing with your emergent reader

BEGINNING READING
Short sentences, familiar words, and simple concepts for children eager to read on their own

READING WITH HELP
Engaging stories, longer sentences, and language play for developing readers

READING ALONE
Complex plots, challenging topics for the independent reader

I Can Read Books have introduced children to the joy of reading since 1957. Featuring award-winning authors and illustrators and a fabulous cast of beloved characters, I Can Read Books set the standard for beginning readers.

A lifetime of discovery begins with the magical words "I Can Read!"

*Visit www.icanread.com for information
on enriching your child's reading experience.*

MOLLY OF DENALI: Little Dog Lost
Copyright © 2019 WGBH Educational Foundation. All rights reserved.

PBS KIDS® and the PBS KIDS logo are registered trademarks of Public Broadcasting Service. Used with permission. All rights reserved.
MOLLY OF DENALI™ is a trademark of WGBH Educational Foundation. Used with permission. All rights reserved.

MOLLY OF DENALI is produced by WGBH Kids and Atomic Cartoons in association with CBC Kids.

Funding for MOLLY OF DENALI is provided by the Corporation for Public Broadcasting and by public television viewers. In addition, the contents of MOLLY OF DENALI were developed under a grant from the Department of Education. However, those contents do not necessarily represent the policy of the Department of Education, and you should not assume endorsement by the Federal Government. The project is funded by a Ready To Learn grant (PR/AWARD No. U295A150003, CFDA No. 84.295A).

www.icanread.com

ISBN 978-0-06-295036-9

Book design by Brenda E. Angelilli and Marisa Rother

20 21 22 23 SCP 10 9 8 7 6 5 4 3 2 1 ❖ First Edition

I Can Read!

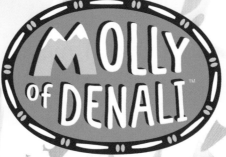

MOLLY OF DENALI™

Little Dog Lost

Based on a television episode written by Mark Zaslove
and Kathy Waugh

HARPER

An Imprint of HarperCollinsPublishers

Hey, everyone, it's Molly!
Today I'm having a fun day
with my friend Tooey
and his dad, Kenji.

We're helping train

Tooey's new sled dog, Anka!

We hear a message on the radio.

"A cold snap is coming, everyone!"

Auntie Midge announces.

It's time to head home,
before it gets too cold out!
Kenji zips away on his snowmobile,
and Tooey and I take the sled.

On the way back,

Tooey's sled hits a snow bank!

We tumble off the sled.

The dogs are all tangled up.

It takes a while to untangle them all.

"Now we just clip Anka back on . . .

Where did Anka go?" Tooey asks.

I look around and see

a set of dog tracks in the snow.

Tooey and I follow the tracks,

but we don't see Anka.

We head back to Tooey's house.

We hope Anka will be there.

But Anka is not at home.

"Don't worry," Kenji says.

"Huskies are built for the cold.

Anka will find shelter tonight.

If she's not home in the morning,

you can go look for her."

The next morning,

Tooey comes to my house.

Anka still is not home.

"Come on, Tooey!" I say.

"We have a dog to find!"

Tooey and I snowshoe to the spot

where our sled crashed.

We look around,

but Anka's tracks are gone!

The wind has erased them.

Luckily, I have a plan.

I take out a box of dog biscuits.

"Let's leave a trail of biscuits

back to your house!" I say.

"If Anka sees the trail,

she'll start eating . . ."

"And end up back home!" says Tooey.

We take turns making a trail.

Soon there are no more biscuits
to build the trail.

"Maybe if we leave our clothes out,
Anka will smell us and know
to keep going," Tooey says.

We make a trail of clothes

all the way to Tooey's house.

Tooey and I wait for hours,
but there is still no sign of Anka!
"I wonder what Anka is doing now,"
Tooey says.

A message comes on the radio.

"Turn your radio up for news!"

says Auntie Midge.

She begins to report today's news.

"That's it!" I say.

"Let's put out a radio message!"

We rush to the radio station.

The radio station

is really just Auntie Midge's house.

I tell Auntie Midge

that Anka is missing.

"Radio's a good way to get out news.

Everyone listens to it,"

says Auntie Midge.

"A good radio message

is short and sweet.

Just like me!" says Auntie Midge.

We write the radio message together.

Tooey makes the announcement.

"I need help finding my dog.

Anka is a red husky.

She has a red and white coat

and a black spot

on her left front paw," he says.

Soon everyone is looking for Anka.

My mom looks by the Trading Post.

Trini and Daniel look by the library.

Grandpa Nat looks down by the lake.

Tooey and I wait to hear
if anyone has seen Anka.
Finally the phone rings.
I pick it up.
"Hello . . . You saw a dog?" I say.

"With a black spot on her paw?

Mahsi'choo!" I say.

That means thank you.

Someone found Anka!

She is back on the trail!

Kenji takes us on his snowmobile
back to the trail in the woods.

Anka is curled up

right on Tooey's scarf!

Tooey runs up and hugs his dog.

"I guess she wanted to stay where she could smell you," says Kenji.

Tooey ties his scarf

around Anka's neck.

"Now you can smell me

ALL the time," Tooey says.

Auntie Midge's Guide to a Perfect Radio Message:

- INTRODUCE YOURSELF!
"Hello, Qyah, this is Tooey . . ."

- EXPLAIN WHAT YOU WANT.
"I need help finding my missing dog . . ."

- BE SPECIFIC . . . BUT NOT TOO SPECIFIC!
"Anka is a red husky. She has a red and white coat and a black spot on her left front paw."

- GIVE IMPORTANT DETAILS!
"Anka got lost near Sooner's Pass last night at sunset. She could be anywhere by now."

- WHAT DO YOU WANT NEXT?
"If you see her, please call Auntie Midge immediately."

- AND ALWAYS BE POLITE . . .
"Mahsi'choo! Thank you!"